HELL'S BOUNTY HUNTER

The Lost Vegas Saga

Kim Cresswell

KC Publishing

For Justin, Carla, Porter, Peyton, and Leo

In memory of Mary Beech

Death leaves a heartache no one can heal,
love leaves a memory no one can steal.
— From a headstone in Ireland

ABOUT THE AUTHOR

Kim Cresswell resides in Ontario, Canada, and is the award-winning author of the action-packed Whitney Steel romantic thriller series.

As a multi-genre author, her books have been featured online at *USA Today*, *NBC*, *FOX*, *Publishers Weekly*, *Booklife*, and *ScifiPulse*.

The Assassin Chronicles TV series was in development with Council Tree Productions. The TV series is based on *Deadly Shadow* and the highly anticipated sequel, *Invisible Truth*.

To learn more about Kim, visit www.kimcresswell.ca

ABOUT HELL'S BOUNTY HUNTER

One minute I was standing at the Gates of Heaven expecting to enter, the next thing I know, I'm thrown down into the Outer Ring of Hell to Level Seven where murderers and others who have committed acts of brutality go.

I'm Chase Decker and I've been coerced into running the bounty hunter division for Lucifer, hunting down rogue demons who've escaped from Hell. My payment? I won't have to suffer the rest of eternity in a vat of hot tar or be tormented by hellhounds.

It sounded like it might be an okay gig until, Layla, the Chief of Evil's daughter disappeared. Rumor has it, that his beautiful offspring plans on forcibly taking over her father's throne with the help of her demon pals.

So much for a quiet afterlife and fresh start to redeem my past. Now, I'm thrust into a new kind of Hell, a vile and dangerous place on Earth called Lost Vegas to find her and drag her home. Did I mention

Lucifer has ordered me to take Hairy Mac, the leather-wearing-talking Dog-God of the Underworld with me?

CHAPTER ONE

I can't stop thinking about being dead.

"This isn't right. I don't belong here," I say with my usual confidence and flick a piece of white fluff off the shoulder of the black designer suit I'm wearing. Across the table, a giant man with a head of thick ginger hair and eyes the color of mustard stares at me. His plastic name badge reads Demon 65390 — Intake Division.

He gives a mirthful laugh. "That's what everyone says when they arrive." His gaze travels to the yellow legal pad clutched in his hands. "Says here, you're Chase Andrew Decker, 34, bounty hunter from Detroit, Michigan. Date of death, October 14, 2023."

Dead cold grips me and I struggle to understand how he knows specific details about me. "For the record, I prefer to be called a Fugitive Recovery Agent. This is a mistake. I was at the Gates of Heaven ready to enter, and something happened. Someone screwed up. They said my name was no longer in the Book of Life."

"That's because you were condemned to eternal Hell for killing Spike Floyd," he says with impatience in his voice.

Everybody's got something they wish they could undo, and this is mine. It's time to face facts. Not only am I in Hell, but there's also a chance I could run into Spike Floyd. I'm screwed. "Come on, seriously. The guy's a king-pin drug dealer, killer, and fugitive. Not your model citizen. Your decision sucks."

"It doesn't matter whether you agree or not. You have a history of making bad choices. Your punishment fits the crime."

A hard knot forms in my stomach. I'm not a friggin saint, but the creep's got it all wrong. I didn't commit a crime. It never went down that way. I took a hit too, for God's sakes, I'm dead. What could be worse than that? Being stuck in Hell forever. I need to get him to listen to me. "I swear it didn't happen like that. It was an accident."

His lifeless eyes connect with mine, and he isn't buying my story even though it's the truth. I may be a lot of things. I'm not a liar.

"You will accept your punishment like everyone else who has entered Hell. Everything is in order."

The full force of my new reality smacks me in the face and anger boils inside me. It's the same seething rage that had gotten me in trouble, to begin with. I desperately want to inflict some bodily harm and make him pay for this horror show but stop myself. "This is a total injustice. I don't belong here."

Looking perturbed, the demon rolls his eyes and tosses the legal pad onto the top of the desk. "You are to report to Level Seven."

Questions plague me as images of pools of fire and hellhounds cycle through my mind. "What's Level Seven?"

"It's where murders and others who have committed acts of brutality end up. Each soul is assigned to a level of the circle, depending on the type of violence they've committed. You'll receive your work assignment from Zila. She may seem like a pushover, don't be fooled. She's tough as nails."

Any hope I had of getting the creature to listen to me, disappeared. I give up on trying to plead my case and turn my attention to the modern office space filled with empty cubicles as far as I can see. Behind me, I'm transfixed by the endless single line of people waiting with empty eyes. Poor bastards. I have no idea how long I've been here since there's no real sense of time.

"There's lots of new arrivals today," the demon says. "It's getting overcrowded."

It's dead silent and the air doesn't reek of sulfur-smelling smoke like I'd been led to believe growing up. What I'm witnessing must be an illusion. This isn't the Hell I was taught about in Sunday School. I'm waiting to hear the sharp lashes of whips, clinking chains, and agonizing screams. Where's the endless abyss of misery, mindless torture, and suffering? Baffled, I scratch my head.

As if reading my mind, he shoots me a look. "Lucifer has modernized many areas of Hell to keep up with the times. Some things have changed, others haven't. We still have many of the classic punishments like burning sand, never-ending icy rain, flaming tombs, and everlasting fire."

Going straight to Hell just took on a new meaning. A work assignment didn't sound half-bad, considering the gruesome and painful alternatives. I mutter "Hallelujah" under my breath, relieved I won't be spending the rest of eternity in a vat of bubbling hot tar.

With a flick of his wrist, the demon motions toward a towering wooden door to my left. "Follow the hall to the end and take the elevator down to Level Seven. Zila's expecting you."

CHAPTER TWO

Still seething about being stuck in Hell, I punch the seventh-floor elevator button. The car descends slowly and then accelerates. A few seconds go by, and the doors ding open. I poke my head out first to make sure there isn't a trap waiting for me. Old habits die hard. All I see is an empty white corridor and a huge blood-red arrow pointing to the right. The air isn't hot or cold, it's just right.

Veering down the corridor, I walk for what seems like forever and finally enter an endless pure white space. There aren't any doors or windows, only emptiness. This is a whole new level of weirdness since demons can mess with your mind and make you see things that aren't there. Am I imagining this or is it real? I can't trust my eyes to tell the difference. An attractive woman around my age with long blond hair to her waist, dressed in skin-tight black leather hot pants and red knee-high boots approaches in true runway style.

She shoots me a smile. "I'm Zila. You must be Chase."

I wanted to give her a witty reply but change my

mind. "Unfortunately."

"Welcome to Hell."

"How long have you been here?"

"About five thousand years. I'm a life harvester, one of Lucifer's deal makers."

"Sounds creepy."

"Not really. I offer favors in exchange for a person's soul. Some of the smart ones know to ask for the life-extension clause to be written in their contract. They devote themselves completely to him."

"I call it insanity." At this point, I'm having a difficult time keeping my eyes off her excessive cleavage. She looks hot for her age. What I'm seeing obviously is not real.

"I know you're skeptical about how things work here."

I burst into laughter. "Lady, that's the understatement of the year."

She steps closer and I notice two things about her. I'm six feet and the woman is taller than me by about three inches. The second is her perfume which smells like gardenias, sandalwood, and soft musk. The scent is familiar, and I recall a girl I used to date years ago who used to wear the same fragrance. Glad I got rid of that one.

"I was skeptical too. It's not that bad. You get used to it." Her tone and body language turn stiff and business-like. "Now, about your work assignment. You will be running Hell's bounty hunter division."

The hairs at the back of my neck stand up, and I

ask what any sane person would ask. "What will I be hunting?"

"Mainly demons who've escaped from Hell. We have another situation on our hands, one which needs immediate attention. Lucifer's daughter, Layla, disappeared four days ago."

The word, 'demon' goes in one ear and out the other. I'm more intrigued by the news of an addition to the King of Hell's family tree. The legacy of evil apparently lives on. "I didn't know he had a daughter."

"It's not something we advertise. Layla is a hybrid. Half demon, half human."

"Why can't Daddy Devil Dearest find her and bring her home? Too busy wreaking havoc and luring mankind into damnation?"

Zila shakes her head. "He can locate her at any time but it's better if he doesn't involve himself since it will only create more tension and resentment between the two."

"What about her mother?"

"We are not allowed to speak about her. For thousands of years, we have dealt with attempted assassinations and uprisings. It's nothing new. We don't need this unfortunate twist. We've been told Layla and her demon friends plan on ousting her father from the throne so that she can take over."

Why would anyone want to rule the worst place in the universe?

"She could be in more danger than she thinks. On the outside, Layla isn't protected. Being part human, she can be killed. She doesn't have the typical demon powers she needs to survive or experience, as most of us do. Layla learned the day before she disappeared that she's a hybrid."

"Guess she didn't take the news well."

"Lucifer's worried the demons she's with could turn on her, erase her from the picture, wanting the throne for themselves. You need to find her quickly and bring her home. Her life is in your hands."

Am I stuck in the worst nightmare or what? None of this can be real. It's unbelievable. I cross my fingers and pray the devil's offspring isn't a child. "How old is she?"

"Thirty-two in human years."

Thank God, I've been spared. I don't mix well with kids. That's why I never had a desire to settle down and have any.

"When a hybrid is born in Hell, there are always signs of the birth in the form of storms, disease outbreaks, or massive power outages."

Remembering how seventy tornadoes had broken out across the United States the year Layla was born, a chill crawls over my skin. "Listen, I'm game for any type of bounty work but hunting down demons and the Princess of Hell, no thanks. Maybe in the next lifetime or when Hell freezes over."

Her blood-red lips tighten, and her voice turns venomous. "You'll do exactly as I say. You lost your right to make choices when you were sentenced for your crime."

I frown. Why is nobody listening to me? How

many times do I have to say I didn't commit a crime? Squaring my shoulders, I tell her what I told the intake demon. "I'm not supposed to be here. Someone screwed up."

"I've heard that one a million times."

"In my case, it's true. I got a raw deal. It was an accident. Besides, I don't know a thing about demons and don't want to."

"I'll teach you everything you need to know. Lucifer has given you some special powers to help you succeed, tricks of the trade."

"Like what?"

"Superhuman speed, strength, and reflexes. Most importantly, you're immune to anything that kills humans."

An icy finger trickles down my spine at the revelation.

"After your formal training, you'll leave for Earth."

I instantly perk up. Now, she's talking. Back to the mortal plane to some normalcy. Anything to get away from this lunacy. "Where am I going?"

"Lost Vegas," she says.

"Don't you mean, **Las Vegas**?"

"Things have changed a lot since you died. Pandemics. World War III. You'll see."

The news makes my stomach curdle. I knew the world was an infectious disease cesspool, and on the verge of war with Russia before I died. Never in my wildest dreams did I think a war would happen. But then again, I never thought I'd end up in Hell. "Why me?"

"You're the best. You've apprehended over ten thousand fugitives."

I'm impressed the woman has gotten my life story correct. My reputation speaks for itself. I'm one of the most successful bounty hunters in the USA. There are a lot of Fugitive Recovery Agents out there who only care about making money. I'm not one of them. I love the job. I'm a thrill junkie. Catching bad guys runs in the family. My father was a bounty hunter for over thirty years before he died of a heart attack eight years ago.

"Things aren't that easy. Nabbing someone is simple. Finding them is harder," I remind her.

"We roughly know where she might be. Lucifer has complete confidence in your ability and talent. Trust me, you don't want to disappoint him." She takes a couple of steps back and folds her hands in front of her. "Let's get started. Stare at me like you want to kill me."

"Is this some sort of freaky hellish foreplay?" I cock my head to one side, bat my lashes, and give her my famous, 'baby-let's-get-down-and-dirty' face.

"Do it," she orders, hissing through her teeth.

Physical excitement builds inside me. No woman as hot as Zila has ever had to ask me for the third time. I'm sure she's a dominatrix. I'm rarely wrong about things like this. My heart rate picks up, and I lick my lips in anticipation waiting for the whip to come out. I stare at her.

Her baby-blues turn into bright red fiery orbs.

I'm wrong, way off about the dominatrix part. What a let-down. My excitement dies, and I take her visual threat seriously in fear of being turned into a pile of smoldering ash. Forcing myself to continue to look at her, pent-up anger explodes, and I feel something else. It's a weird itchy sensation in the center of my spine between my shoulders. A loud, sharp pop, followed by ruffling takes me by surprise.

My gaze snaps over my shoulder and I see a set of giant black wings curving up, towering above me. "What the fuck?" Slapping and punching at the movable objects of flight, feathers fly in every direction like a busted open pillow and float down around me. "Get these things off me."

"I can't. They're part of you. They're a gift, a lovely addition."

Shocked, I can't think straight. I get in her face and yell, "Eff you! I never asked for them. I don't want them!"

Minutes go by, and I stop thrashing at the ridiculous change forced on my body. When I finally calm down, the wings flutter in slow gentle waves and swoosh around me. I reach and run my fingers along the spine of the feathers. It feels like muscles and bones.

Zila laughs. "How else did you think you were going to get to Earth?"

"How about time travel, magic, or maybe a snap of your demon ass fingers?" I say in a sarcastic tone. "You could have warned me."

She shakes her head and grins. "No way. It was

too much fun watching your reaction. You were screaming like a little girl."

More and more I want to flee this endless life freak show and then realize I can. I've hit the jackpot. The wings are a blessing, my ticket out of here. "How do I get rid of them, put them back where they came from?"

"It's simple. Use your anger to make them appear and will your mind to make them disappear."

I focus and try it. The wings collapse and vanish. I test it out a few more times for good measure.

"Before I teach you how to fly, I have someone I want you to meet." She holds out her arm as if she's presenting a prize on a game show.

A gigantic muscular dog ripped like a cartoon character, emerges out of nowhere like an apparition and gallops toward us. A blur of black fur and red beaming eyes race at me. You have got to be kidding. The monster looks like a mutated furry Doberman-Great Dane. My eyes travel to his paws as big as my hand. The animal circles me once, sniffing, then sits at Zila's side.

Stroking the top of the dog's head with long red painted nails, Zila says, "This is Hairy Mac, Dog-God of the Underworld. Lucifer has ordered you to take our very special boy with you to find and bring Layla home. You will work as a team."

"I'm not a team player. No way, dogs aren't my thing. I'm allergic." That part is true. I have been since I was five years old. Rabbits too.

"Don't worry, any past medical problems you had,

died with you."

I hold up a hand in frustration, half expecting a heavenly intervention to save me from this freak show. "I only work alone. Those are my rules."

Zila's face twists with a mix of amusement and annoyance. "This isn't a negotiation. Although your resistance is cute and charming, and even a turn-on, it won't get you anywhere in Hell.

* * *

Later that day, the heels of my shoes touch the ground, and I'm relieved I made a perfect landing after maneuvering the wild currents and violent updrafts. It was exhilarating and I feel alive. Hours of practicing interdimensional flying sure came in handy. Sucking in a lungful of fresh air, the warmth of the sun touches my skin and feels good. I'm ecstatic to be back in the land of the living, far away from the infernal pit of punishment. My aerodynamic wings snap shut behind me and I'm still amazed by the cool parlor trick. It's superhero kind of stuff. I could get used to this type of traveling, now that I've gotten the hang of it. Being dead, on the other hand, is going to take a lot longer to sink in if it ever does.

Determined to first hit a bar and have a drink before getting to work on tracking down Lucifer's daughter, I straighten my jacket and spot a used condom stuck to the heel of one of my thousand-dollar leather shoes. Grimacing, I pick up the rubber with two fingers and toss the thing into the putrid overflowing Dumpster a few steps away, wishing I had a bottle of disinfectant in my pocket. Beside me, I see Hairy Mac in all his glory. He has the same black wings except mine are spectacular and glamorous. His are lopsided, dull, and missing feathers. I blink hard and squint. Is he wearing a leather jacket and boots? Good Lord, he is. All I can do is chuckle at the ridiculous sight.

Glancing around, I recognize I'm in the middle of Naked City in western Lost Vegas. Usually, I have a good sense of direction but this time my landing coordinates are off by six or seven blocks. During my previous visits to the city, cab drivers refused to come to this area at night, for fear of being robbed or worse. With nerve endings on high alert and armed with a Ruger P89 9 mm in my shoulder holster under my jacket, I sense a violent undertone heavy in the air. I glance at my Rolex to make sure I still have some time before it gets dark. Luckily, it's still early, only three in the afternoon.

On exiting the alley, in the distance, the towering Stratosphere at the end of the strip catches my eye. I imagine hearing the thrill rides and dings, whistles, and bells of thousands of slot machines in my head coming from downtown. Three cop cars race by with their sirens blaring and kick up a filthy cloud of dust in my face. I get a nasty whiff of the fecal-smelling massive tent city across the street occupied by hundreds of homeless people. There's a lot of fighting, yelling, and gunshots, stuff I want to stay clear of. I'm not interested in making any enemies. Turning the corner, I keep my head down and walk six more blocks, staying within the shadows. The screwball dog is hot on my heels, panting and grunting.

Ducking into the only bar I find; The Island Tap isn't much to look at from the outside with its rusting wrought-iron bars over the windows. Inside, the place is dimly lit and lacking any form of air conditioning or tasteful decorating. As I glance around, I remember reading somewhere that Tiki bars had gone out of style after World War II. A heavily tattooed man wearing a red and white Hawaiian print shirt and khaki chino shorts is behind the bar wiping glasses with a rag. His head snaps up when I approach.

"You sure don't look like you're from around here," the guy says with a British accent and gives me the once over.

It wasn't the warm welcome I was expecting. I take a seat at the bar on an uneven wooden stool and realize I'm severely overdressed for the neighborhood. Another thing hits me. I'm wearing the same suit I probably was buried in. Sadness washes over me and my thoughts turn to my mother. It must have been difficult for her to pick out the perfect outfit, knowing how important it was to me to be impeccably dressed. When this gig is done, I'll stop by and make sure she's okay. Grief is a horrible thing. I know she must miss her only child. We were pretty tight. I miss her too.

"Where you from?" The bartender asks, wiping the sweat from his forehead.

"Detroit," I tell him, knowing the guy isn't going to believe I flew in from Hell.

"Here on business or pleasure?"

"Business." I pull out the photograph of Layla that Zila had given me from my breast pocket and hold it up. "I'm looking for someone. Have you seen her?"

He shakes his head. "Good-looking girl. If money is no object, check The Tempest Frontier Casino & Resort. It's the 'in' hangout for the wealthy crowd since the war. Otherwise, she could be in the tunnels or at one of the two dozen tent cities the government set up."

"I doubt she's gone underground. She definitely likes the finer things in life." Before putting the photo back in my pocket, I find myself staring at Layla's long red hair and vibrant turquoise eyes. She's a stunning woman with a face and body a man can't forget. Something stirs in me, a deep physical attraction to a woman I've never met.

"Wife or girlfriend?" the bartender asks.

"Neither."

"You're a long way from home." He sets down a glass and gestures to the dog. "What's up with the mutt?"

I was wondering how long it would take before he mentioned the elephant in the room.

"I can't believe he's wearing a studded leather jacket and matching boots." He lets out a deep belly laugh. "That's the craziest thing I've ever seen."

I glance at Hairy Mac sitting next to me. He

looks more like he's ready to party at a club than the evil Dog-God of the Underworld. How can anybody take him seriously? He's snarling and showing his brownish-black teeth. It's bad enough his thousand-year-old rancid breath reeks like rotting ass, I worry this isn't going to end well for the bartender if he keeps making fun of the canine. Not wanting any trouble, I order a drink and something to eat. "I'll have a Jack Daniels, make it a double, straight up and I'll take a cheeseburger, and fries."

The man is barely able to stifle his laughter. "Anything for your sidekick?"

I hear a high-pitched voice say, "Water and a shot of your best Tequila."

Twisting my head back and forth, I'm convinced I'm losing my mind. The bar is empty other than the three of us, a broken jukebox, and the horrendous bamboo and fake grass decor. My gaze snaps like an elastic band to the dog, and then to the bartender. "Did you hear that?"

He arches a brow and passes our food order to the cook, a short man with tattoos of rattlesnakes on both forearms. "Hear what?"

Only one thing makes sense. It's the furry vile creature talking! My jaw drops open in disbelief. Zila had mentioned the dog was special but...he can talk? How is it possible?

Demon-dog paws my leg and digs his biker boot into my left thigh hard enough to make me shift on the stool. "Asshole, I'm right here. I can hear what you're saying and thinking."

I hide my shock and order him what he wants, afraid he'll take a chunk out of my leg or worse. "Bring him a bowl of water and a shot of your best Tequila. Better bring him a cheeseburger too."

The bartender's eyes double in size at my request. "Does he have a name?"

I nod. "This is Hairy Mac, Dog-God of the Underworld."

He starts to mumble something, instead turns, and quietly gets our drinks.

At that moment, I question whether I am bat-shit crazy. Turns out, I'm fully certifiable. I'm dead, sitting in a Tiki bar in a five-thousand-dollar suit with a leather-clad talking dog ordering him a shot of booze and a burger. If that isn't crazy, I don't know what is.

After downing my drink, I pour the Tequila into the bowl of water and give it to the dog. He laps it up and appears satisfied. While I'm waiting on the food, I notice a copy of the *Las Vegas Sun* on the bar, a stool away from me. I pick it up and observe the date: October 14, 2027. I stop stone-cold. Four years have gone by. Where have I been all this time?

"Hello, news flash, asshole. You were in purgatory, the tormented abyss, waiting to be purified for Heaven. Lucifer pulled you from Heaven's gates at the last minute because he needed an experienced bounty hunter. Now, I'm stuck with you. Oh, goody."

The truth is tough for me to hear. Fragmented images flash through my brain.

Chasing Spike Floyd with the bond agreement, arrest warrant, and mugshot on the seat beside me...ramming his truck with mine...plummeting down a ravine...glass shattering...smoke...fire...

I remember a quiet calm and feeling an immense amount of torment like being suspended in mental agony. I shouldn't have run him off the road. It was a bad decision. I screwed up. I let my anger control me. Obviously, it didn't end well for either of us. I push the memories away, growing more irritated by the dog's voice that sounds like he swallowed a bag of squeaky toys. "I was right. It was a mistake. I was supposed to go to Heaven. I'm not a bad guy after all."

"If you say so, buddy."

"Don't call me that. I'm not your buddy, friend, or anything else."

Minutes later, the bartender clears his throat and puts the plates of food in front of me. "Do you always talk to him?"

It isn't going to matter what I say. The guy already thinks I'm a total whack-job. "Believe me, only when I have to."

Ready to dig into my food, the delectable aroma of beef and onions travels to my nostrils. Starving, I shove a couple of French fries in my mouth, then take a huge bite of the burger, savoring every morsel. Grabbing the plate with the other cheeseburger, I place it on the floor. The dog snatches the food and gulps it down then lets out a loud burp.

Still determined to work alone, I mull over getting the dog pass-out-drunk and ditching him until after I find Layla. But a frightening low growl erupts from the beast, reminding me that pissing off the Dog-God is not in my best interest.

CHAPTER THREE

Heading down W Flamingo Road toward The Tempest Frontier Casino & Resort, I glance in a window and recognize my face. For a dead guy, I look the same as I did before I died: Tall, blue-eyed, and handsome. Running my hand through my dark brown hair, I check out my rugged face and square jaw. A block up, I stop at a clothing store to grab some necessities. Fifteen minutes later, I put on a pair of mirrored aviator shades and exit the store armed with two shopping bags overflowing with my purchases. Hairy Mac is sitting in the middle of the sidewalk.

"Took you long enough," he says.

I walk at a brisk pace, trying to put some distance between myself and the whiny beast. No such luck. "Man, you've got a lot to say. It's not normal for a dog to talk. You're a freak of nature."

He stops in front of me, and his eyes erupt into fiery red torches. He gives a terrorizing growl and shows his true ghastly hideous form, a mass of bone, blood, and flames. I feel as if the air is being sucked out of my lungs. Gasping, the intense hatred projected at me is overwhelming like I'm being sucked into a vortex of pure evil. The mental pain in my head is too much. Shaking and scared shitless, I'm unable to speak.

"Have I got your attention, asshole?"

A few long beats pass before I can form any type of coherent thought or sentence. I think I just survived some crazy kind of demon possession. Finally able to breathe again, I find my voice. "We'll check into the resort and hit the casino. From what Zila told me, Layla won't be able to stay away from anything rich, especially high rollers."

I keep my eyes straight ahead and walk around him, not wanting to witness what I just saw ever again. I'm having a hard enough time understanding the immense poverty and homelessness. It's a thousand times worse than before I died. No wonder this place is called Lost Vegas. It's Hell on Earth.

"After the war, inflation pushed people into poverty," the dog says, trotting beside me. "Humans aren't too bright. They're always destroying their world."

"Did we at least win the war?" I ask, swatting a swarm of gnats around my head.

"Look around, what do you think? There aren't any winners. Unprecedented job losses and global starvation that has never been seen on Earth before, have forced the power-wealthy to continue to thrive. You're either dead, rich, or impoverished. Or you're me."

I can't believe what I'm hearing or seeing. The

city for the most part is a slum, a cesspit of despair. There are cops on every corner, rundown, and abandon buildings. Garbage is everywhere.

Rounding the corner, I pass a gray-haired old man in ragged and torn clothing sitting on a milk crate. He glares at me. On the streets, you never know who's a friend or enemy. I'm on guard, overly cautious, and still a bit shaky after seeing the dog's true form, something I can't seem to unsee. I hear scurrying, like overgrown nails clawing the pavement and I flinch. Three rats the size of a small dog scramble across the street in front of me. In a brief instant two dudes in Hoodies and baggie jeans with cloth skull masks covering their mouths and noses leap out of the narrow alley between two buildings.

Great. Just what I need. Hoodlums. I take a deep breath and let it out slowly. I've learned to remain cool and calm in the most difficult situations and this is one of them. It comes with the territory. I stop, wishing I had changed out of my suit when I was in the store because this is going to get messy.

I hear the dog ask, "Friends of yours?"

"Shut up," I tell him.

The taller dude shoves the barrel of a Glock in my face. Big mistake.

"Who are you telling to shut up? Gimme your wallet and the rollie." Eyeballing the dog, the man snort-laughs. "What kind of mutt is that?"

"The kind that can rip your arms and legs off then crush your skull with one bite."

He freezes for a second, then wraps his other hand around the handle of the gun. "Mr. Fancy-Schmancy, I ain't scared of no dog. He's gotta be dumb as dirt dressed like that." He jerks the gun closer, an inch from my forehead. "Gimme your wallet and watch. I ain't asking again."

The other dude is oblivious to what's going on. He's in his own world, shaking, jacked up on speed or crystal meth, twitching like a marionette. There's no way I'm parting with my watch. I worked years to get one. It cost me eighty grand. Dropping the shopping bags to the ground, I wait for the dog to make the first move. He acts as if he's deaf, lifts his leg, and pisses on the corner of the building.

"My money's on the hoodlums," the beast says and lowers his leg.

Now, who's the asshole. Focusing, I squash down my anger to stop my wings from making an impromptu appearance and narrow my eyes at the guy with the gun. Part of me wants him to shoot me to prove I can't be killed. I could have easily pulled out my weapon and double-tapped both men in the head.

With jackrabbit reflexes, I sidestep the gun-toting dude. Within seconds, I have the gun out of his hands and pointed it at him. Normally, I'm fast but not like this. The special powers Lucifer gave me are awesome. It's as if I'm supercharged, able to move faster, and I'm stronger than ever. Pocketing the weapon, it's time to open a can of whoop-ass on the two fools and I don't hold back. I come at them full force.

After a couple of solid right jabs and a nice left hook to the gunslinger's face, I wheel around, lift my leg, and thrust my heel directly into his tweaking friend's chest, knocking him off his feet. It feels good to hurt someone and these guys deserve it. The men retreat, bloodied, and stumble away in the opposite direction.

Picking up my bags I continue walking, irate that the dog purposely tuned me out when all he had to do was show his real self to the men. If he had, I wouldn't have sore and bruised knuckles. "Thanks for the help."

"Not my job."

"What exactly is your job?" I groan in response. "Strutting around town showing off your ludicrous doggie outfit? In case you didn't know, it's not fall fashion week."

"You need me, smart-ass. I can sniff out demons, something you can't do. That's why I'm here."

This is news to me. Knowing who's a demon will come in handy since Zila had mentioned Layla has a couple of them accompanying her. "Are you going to have my back next time?"

"Sure thing. I'm here to serve you."

"I don't believe you," I say coldly, picking up my pace a bit. "Can I show my true self and scare people too?"

"Only demons in Lucifer's close inner circle can. You aren't one of us and you never will be. You aren't worthy."

"Why do you have to be such a condescending jerk? I bet you were taken away from your mother too young and dropped on your head. Explains why you're such a bundle of joy to be around."

Fangs clamp down on my forearm and I feel each dagger-sharp tooth pierce my suit jacket and graze my skin.

"If you know what's good for you, don't mention my mother again. She's perfect in every way."

"Let go of me. You seriously need to attend some anger management classes. You're way too sensitive for a dog. I didn't mean to hurt your feelings."

A few seconds go by, and the beast releases my arm, leaving giant noticeable holes in the arm of my jacket. When I think I can't be more disgusted, he stops and goes about his business in the shadows of the resort's two towers. I'm talking turd the size of a giant pile of horse crap. "Do you have to do that right here so close to the entrance?" I let out a sigh and keep my distance since I'm standing downwind. When he's done, he kicks his feet behind him like he's running on the spot.

The outside of the resort is lit up by the old Las Vegas standards, The Neon Capital of the World. Walking past one of the valets out front, climbing into a black Maserati Ghibli, I make my way to the entrance of the resort and notice four rent-a-cops in heavy black body armor, armed with assault rifles. When I'm about to open the door, one of them stops me and puffs out his chest. "No pets allowed."

I give him the side eye and say the first thing

that pops into my mind. "He's my emotional support dog."

He looks at the dog then at me and laughs. "You need more than emotional support because you're blind as a bat if you think it's okay to dress him like that. There's a doggy daycare next door for our guests."

"Thanks." I move a few yards away from him and ask Hairy Mac, "Now what?"

"Doggy daycare is for sissies. It's not happening."

"Why not? You might meet a hot Poodle, the doggy of your dreams."

"I get more than enough action, thanks."

"That's not something I needed to know. You could stay out here, and I could go in alone."

"Nice try. I'm not letting you out of my sight. You have a job to do, and so do I. I'll find a body to take over."

My pulse speeds up. "You can do that?"

"I'm a demon. I can do anything Lucifer can, like ripping out your jugular just because I don't like you."

"Believe me, the feeling is mutual," I mutter to myself.

Not wanting to anger him again, I scan the valet's covered area and spot a stocky dude with a salt-and-pepper comb-over getting out of a dark blue McLaren F1. My pulse speeds up at the sight of the sweet ride. You can tell a lot about a man by his car and his shoes. The guy is screaming high-roller with his heavy gold chains and three-thousand-dollar

Blue Crocodile cowboy boots. I point to the guy. "What about him?"

Hairy Mac takes off running, pounces in the air and disintegrates into the back of the man's body like magic. I'm blown away. I wasn't expecting him to pull a David Copperfield right in front of me. Impressive. Hate to admit I'm jealous I can't do the same thing. He saunters back to me awkwardly in his brand-new demon body, adjusting his neck a few times.

"I like this one," he says. "It suits me. Fits well."

When he speaks, I detect a Texan drawl. Thank God he has a big-boy voice now because if I had to listen to him squeak-talking any longer, I'd go and jump off a tall building. "We'll get a room in case we have to stay for a few days. Hopefully, Layla's here."

He nudges me in the ribs then grabs his crotch with both hands. "Whoa, check this out. This guy's got a huge one."

I roll my eyes unable to keep my disgust hidden by his public display and walk ahead of him pretending I've never seen him before in my life.

* * *

The resort is massive, much bigger than I remember. While Harry Mac is sniffing a potted tree beside a half-moon-shaped bar, I'm worried he'll lift his leg, or worse, start humping a guest's leg, forgetting he's in human form.

At the front desk, a glamorous long-haired brunette gives me a movie-star-worthy smile. Her intense green eyes meet mine. "Welcome to The Tempest Frontier Casino & Resort."

I return the smile, and slap down the Amex Black card with unlimited credit, Zila had given me on the counter. "I'll take the best suite you've got."

"That would be our nine-thousand-square-foot-two-story villa, the most luxe suite in the world."

"How much?"

"It's one hundred thousand dollars a night."

I feel a rush of giddy excitement at the thought of blowing the King of Hell's cash on the best room in the house. Pure justice. Payback is a bitch. "I'll take it."

"How long will you be staying with us?" she asks and runs her tongue slowly over her top lip in a sexual kind of way.

"Check me in for two nights," I tell her.

"The suite includes a ten-thousand-dollar credit, A-list access to the open-air rooftop Aqua Lounge and Nightclub in tower two, plus in-suite twenty-four-hour butler service."

The last thing I want is another body around, day and night. It's going to be bad enough with the dog. "You can cancel the butler service. I won't need it."

She nods and peers over the counter. "Do you have any luggage you need taken up?"

I hold up my two shopping bags and pause for effect. "I think I can handle it."

She hands back the Amex card and I put it in my pocket.

"You'll be on the sixtieth floor, tower one. Here's

your key card. I hope you enjoy your stay." Tucking a strand of loose hair behind her ear, she leans in close enough for me to feel her breath against my cheek and slides a black and gold card in my hand. "If you need any personal attention later, give me a call. My shift ends in an hour."

I glance down at the card and the name on it reads Jenny Favor. She's not your typical Jenny-from-the-block. In my line of work, I've seen it all. She's a call girl, the kind that fetches up to eight-hundred bucks an hour. A switch goes off in my head and I get a wild idea. Opportunity always knocks when you least expect it. Jenny Favor could keep Hairy Mac busy for a few hours while I make my rounds in the casino to find Layla. I doubt he'd pass on getting laid, after all, he's a dog. Maybe she'll teach the old demon a few new tricks. I slip the card into my pocket.

Leaving the reception counter, I swear I smell crazy in the air and my instincts are dead on. A few hundred feet away, a group of guests are gathered around Hairy Mac. He's sniffing a dwarf palm tree across from a busy upscale steakhouse. All eyes are on him. As I get closer, I hear someone ask, "Is he alright? Should we call security?"

Hiring Jenny Favor is sounding better by the minute. I move in fast to defuse the situation. "Sorry folks. He's off his meds. I need to get him back to the psych ward."

As the onlookers disperse with wide eyes and shaking heads, I grab Hairy Mac's arm and escort him toward the glass elevators. My patience snaps.

"You can't be sniffing everything like a crazy dog. In here, you're human. Act like one. You're going to get us kicked out."

"I caught the scent of a demon," he informs me.

"Seriously? Just by sniffing?"

"And you thought I was going to take a leak in front of everyone."

I don't answer him. The conversation is pointless other than the part about a demon. I wonder if Layla's chums know we're here. My first bounty hunting gig needs to go without a hitch to stay on Lucifer's good side. I refuse to think about the alternative.

"If I can smell them, they can smell me," he says, reading my mind. "They know we're here."

"This isn't a 'we' situation," I point out. "I'm not an evil supernatural being like you. I'm just a dead guy railroaded from Heaven and forced into Hell." In the elevator, the tension in the air is thick as fog. "I have nothing to worry about, right?"

"Don't kid yourself."

"What does that mean?"

He snickers. "If you run into a demon, you're going to get the ass-kicking of all eternity."

Worry gnaws at my gut. "Are you trying to scare me? You promised to have my back."

"I never promised anything."

"You're such a dick. I thought you were here to serve me. Those are **your** words, not mine." The elevator doors open, and he gives me a ball-breaking stare. I drop it. It's not worth arguing with him.

Stepping into a grand foyer with gray and black flecked marble floors and matching walls leading to the suite's door, I pull the key card out of my pocket and give it a swipe. The door automatically opens into a mind-blowing space that reeks of serious coin and luxury. I drop my shopping bags at my feet.

The open-concept villa is exquisitely decorated in silver and black paint with splashes of aquamarine and has colorful butterflies inlaid on the marble floors. Even the sleek industrial furniture and abstract art on the walls must be worth a fortune. The place is way over-the-top. "So, this is what a hundred grand a night buys. Cool."

"Lucifer is going to boil you in tar and strip the skin from your bones for spending so much money."

I look at him and his comb-over is sticking up revealing freckled smooth skin. "Let's not get side-tracked from what matters. He wants his daughter back and this is the cost of doing business."

"We could've stayed at the Motel 6."

"And give up the life of the rich and famous plus a vacay away from Hell?" I pour a double shot of Jack at the curved twelve-seat bar and suck it back in one swallow. "Zila never told me how to protect myself if I get caught up with a demon."

"The gun you're packing isn't going to do much."

"Then how? Enlighten me."

"You need bullets crafted from a melted-down archangel blade. They'll kill most demons."

"Most? What aren't you telling me?"

"It depends on the hierarchy of the demon."

I fight back a grin. "Can the bullets kill **you**?"

"You wish." Hairy Mac shoves both hands down the front of his pants and rummages around his crotch like he's digging to China.

"Man, what are you doing?"

He pulls out his hands and four shiny silver bullets. Holding them out to me, I hesitate, contemplating if I should touch them. Cringing, I take them.

"Don't say I never gave you anything, asshole." He brushes past me to the terrace and jumps into the oversize cantilevered Jacuzzi fully clothed as if it's a swimming pool.

Glancing at the bullets, I want to remove the skin from my hands with a wire brush in fear of catching something gnarly from him. After checking out the numerous fish and shark tanks, gym, and movie theater, I make my way upstairs and take a hot shower, overjoyed to rid my hand of any nasty bacteria. When I'm done, I get dressed, slap on a lavish designer cologne supplied by the resort and give Jenny Favor a call. I ask her to bring some weed to help fun-the-night-up for Hairy Mac. He won't know what hit him. I have no problem parting with a couple of thousand bucks for her time when it's on Lucifer's dime. It'll be worth every penny to keep the dog occupied so I can do my job, alone. There's no doubt in my mind that demon-dog is going to make me pay for heading out on my own. I have to find Layla and fast. The last thing I want is to end up as a skinned mannequin nailed to a wall behind Lucifer's throne.

"...Is your friend into anything kinky?" Jenny purrs on the other end of the phone.

"He's quite the little demon, a real beast. The kinkier, the better."

"I'm on my way," she says and hangs up.

CHAPTER FOUR

An hour after Jenny Favor arrived at the suite, I escape undetected, leaving the party of two as high as a kite and the Do Not Disturb sign on the door. It's a godsend. I feel like the master of my own universe. Freedom smells good. Heading downstairs decked out in a white button-up shirt, black jeans, and black leather jacket, I'm eager to see if Layla is here.

Strolling into the casino, the security presence is heavy, like nothing I ever witnessed when I was alive. My muscles tense. There aren't any windows to know if it's still daylight, only the constant sound of slot machines, spinning, ringing, and dinging.

A call girl by the name of Sugar Pop with a neon-blue pixie-cut and a pink feather boa wrapped around her shoulders, hands me her card. I refrain from making a smart-ass comment about her stiletto-shaped fingernails and deposit the card into my jacket pocket until I can find a trash can. I've never paid for sex and I'm not about to start. Since becoming a Fugitive Recovery Agent, women flock to me and throw themselves at my feet like I'm a cop or something. I'm a rockstar bounty hunter, a badass.

Stalking through the maze of machines, rich older women with painted-on brows and eyelashes stiff with heavy black mascara gawk at me as if I'm the special on tonight's menu. Unable to shake the image of Layla from my mind, I stop and check every woman with red hair, and eye each male with suspicion. Anyone of them could be a demon. How would I know for sure?

Before moving on to the poker rooms, I order a Jack Daniel's from a cute college-aged server in a skimpy pink halter top and matching micromini skirt. With my drink in hand, I'm troubled by what I'm witnessing. The casino looks more like an underground private club for deep-pocketed gamblers in designer attire dripping in gold and diamonds while most of the city's desolate souls fight for survival.

Concerned my wings will emerge, I quickly bury my anger at the economic disparity and head into the first poker room to find every table jammed with big spenders and non-stop drinks being served. I quickly survey the female crowd. Disappointed Layla isn't here, I explore the next room and the next. Four drinks later, I rub a hand over my face and enter the Encore Room, lavishly decorated in royal red and gold, fit for kings and queens. The air is electrified with energy.

In the far corner, standing beside an Italian Stallion who'd pass as a male stripper seated at one of the oval tables playing blackjack, I spot her. My heart skips a beat. It's a miracle of all miracles. The Princess of Darkness is absolutely breathtaking, the way her flawless creamy skin shimmers under the lights. I force myself to breathe. Attempting to get a better view, I move across from her, a few tables away, and pretend to watch another card game. My attention is glued to the two bald scumbags, twins, standing behind her. One of them has a jagged scar running down the left side of his face. They look like genies in their white shirts and suits. I peg them as demons. I hope I'm right.

Watching her big-spender-friend bet twenty-thousand dollars against the dealer's cards, I notice he has almost a quarter of a million bucks in chips stacked in front of him, guarded by two rent-a-cops and the male pit boss overseeing the game. Next problem. How do I get Layla away from her demon pals and out of the casino without causing a ruckus? I have a feeling in the pit of my gut that this job isn't going to be as easy as I thought.

When a server comes by, I order another double Jack and a glass of Dom Pérignon for Layla, in hopes of catching her eye. While I'm watching her, I remember my father's words.

"If you can't nab them right away, engage them in conversation to gain their trust."

Those same words had helped me bag some of the most dangerous bail-skippers of all time that no one else could catch. Not even the FBI.

Once I have my drink, I lean against the wall, take a sip, and observe the server delivering the glass of champagne on a round gold tray to Layla like she's royalty. Unsure of her reaction or the response of her creepy companions, anticipation rocks my nerves and my heart pounds. Her vivid turquoise eyes slowly sweep the room and finally lock on mine. She smiles and holds up her glass. I raise my drink and flash my best smile.

Minutes later, the Italian Stallion loses his hand, stands up, his features tight with anger, and hastily collects his chips. He pushes Layla out of the way and brushes past me. The two rent-a-cops follow him.

One problem down. Two to go.

I finish my drink and walk toward her, my eyes lingering on her beauty. Fluffing her long hair, her gaze never leaves mine as she approaches.

She's about five-foot-eight, dressed in a sexy short black cocktail dress and clear transparent high heels that show off her shapely slender legs. Meeting me halfway, I become deaf and blind to the world around me. The strong chemistry between us is like nothing I've experienced before. It's a magnetic pull that makes me want to protect her, take her under my wings, literally. I give myself a mental shake and face reality. I can't get involved with her. Lucifer will remove my balls and feed them to Hairy Mac for dinner. A ripple of fear travels through me at the grisly thought.

"Thanks for the glass of Dom," she says as a wicked smile crosses her lips. "I'm Layla. Do you come here often?"

She's undressing me with those magnificent round eyes, and I can't fight the attraction no matter how hard I try. My heart flip-flops. I'm doomed, mesmerized by her sultry voice, and selfishly want more. As my gaze drops to her pink-tinted lips, I turn on the charm and lower my voice to sound sexier. "Not as often as I'd like. I'm Chase. How about we get a cozy booth, a bottle of Dom, and some dinner?"

Something flashes in the back of her eyes and sets alarm bells off in my head. The twins step closer to her in unison, one on either side of her. Something stinks, isn't right. I try to stay calm. From what Zila had told me, Layla had come to Lost Vegas to round up more support to overthrow her father with the help of demons who had escaped from Hell. That isn't the vibe I'm getting from her. She's scared.

"Who's your friends?" I ask, attempting to keep the conversation going for as long as possible.

She glances at the twins and then back at me. "I better get back to my room. Thanks for the champagne."

Feeling a rush of despair in her tone, I grab her hand, and a firestorm of sensations breaks out when our skin touches. It's the first real thing I've felt since I died. "Come on, a girl's got to eat. Steak or seafood or both? Whatever you want."

One of the twin-clowns moves in front of her and jabs a thick finger at my chest. A muscle flicks angrily at his jaw.

I release Layla's hand.

"Get lost." He pushes me with both hands, back

a few steps and I bump into the edge of one of the poker tables. No one at the table notices or says anything.

My spine stiffens. I don't like being pushed around. I've knocked out guys for less and this guy is asking for it. "Let the lady decide what she wants to do."

The other twin, Scarface, doesn't appreciate my straightforwardness. He gets in my personal space, standing toe to toe with me in a staring contest. His chin is rough with stubble and his dark eyes are glazed over, looking as if they might burst into flames. "Get out of the way. The woman is going to her room."

Waving a dismissive hand in the air, I blurt out, "Hit the road, Jack. This is a private party between me and the lady. You and your boyfriend aren't invited."

Scarface's eyes harden, and I realize it was a bad idea, my usual habit of speaking before, I think. Planting his monster-sized palms against my chest, he shoves me backward, and I land in the lap of a silver-haired elderly woman with smeared red painted lips.

Grandma waggles her drawn-on brows and caresses my arm. Then she plants a sloppy kiss on my cheek.

I bounce to my feet. I'm freaking out a bit at the thought of shooting the demons inside the casino. I work out my options in my head. If I do, Layla will know her father sent me. I can't. Not yet. I need to get to know her. There's an unspoken connection between us that is seriously messing with my mind and heart. I never expected to feel this way. If I can spend an hour with her before I take her back to her father, it's better than nothing. I make my choice and steel myself for what's to come.

The anticipated punch doesn't happen. Instead, Scarface grabs Layla's arm roughly, manhandling her, and drags her toward the door. She glances over her shoulder, and I spot fear in her eyes.

My fingers curl into fists and the damn wings are going to come out whether I want them to or not. I yank out my gun and yell, "Stop!"

Instantaneously, reality blurs. I swear someone is behind me breathing down the back of my neck. Then I sense a nasty wave of crazy in the air and things turn super weird.

* * *

Strangling the handle of the gun with two hands, I blink over and over and hear my wings snap open like a pop-tent. What just happened? When my vision clears, I look around. Gamblers, servers, and dealers are magically incapacitated, suspended in time like statues. My jaw drops open.

One guy has a finger stuffed up his nose and Grandma's holding an open tube of red lipstick ready to tackle another layer. I pry a drink out of one of the server's hands and knock it back in a single gulp. Holstering my gun, my heart sinks. Layla is nowhere in sight, and neither are the twins.

I run to the door leading to the slot machines and my wings get jammed up on both sides of the doorframe. I fly backward off my feet. Flat on my back, I look up. Hairy Mac is hulking over me, still in human form, like the grim reaper, pinning me down with a threatening gaze. His red eyes aren't glowing, yet.

I turn my head, not wanting a repeat performance of his real self. "You did this. Layla's gone. She was right here."

"You disobeyed Zila. We're a team," he says with an angry growl.

There's an edge in his voice, that I know all too well. I take his cue and clamp my mouth shut. About to sit up, the sole of a size thirteen cowboy boot comes down hard on the center of my chest and stops me. "For Christ's sakes, let me up."

A couple of minutes pass before he bends down and wraps one hand around my neck, almost strangling me. He raises me high in the air and lowers me to the floor.

Coughing until I catch my breath, I shoot him a nasty look. "You could've just let me get up without the ridiculous demon theatrics."

"You have lipstick on your face."

I wipe my cheek with the back of my hand and look around. "Where's your friend, Jenny Favor?"

"Dead," he says with cold-blooded calm.

"What?"

"You heard me."

"You killed her?"

"Not on purpose."

"What do you mean, not on purpose?"

He blinks a few times and looks away.

My stomach drops. "What have you done?"

"If you have to know, we were having sex for the twenty-fifth time and—"

"Are you serious? Twenty-five times in less than an hour and a half? Good God man, you killed the poor girl with your dick. Unbelievable." Panic courses through me at the thought of housekeeping discovering the body and then the cops hunting us down.

"You're such a worrywart. I dumped her at the tent city down the street. Ever watch the movie, *Weekend at Bernie's*? It was easy-peasy getting her out of the resort."

A talking dog who watches movies. What next? I need to get out of KookyVille before I lose my friggin mind. I give my head a shake and focus on what's important. "We don't have time for this. We need to find Layla. I think her demon friends are using her. I'm just not sure how. She doesn't want to take over Lucifer's throne. It's them. They want to rule Hell."

"How do you know this?" he asks.

"I'm a good read of people."

"You misread me."

"You're a dog, not a person. Can we stop wasting time?" My wings collapse and I hurry out the door to the slot machines where every living being is suspended in the last position they were in before time stopped. The game *Twister* comes to mind.

"That's a cool trick. How do you do it? Does it last long?"

"You ask too many questions."

"My mother calls it inquisitive."

"As long as I need it to last. It's a little trick I learned from Uriel, an archangel. The 'how' is for demon ears only."

"The least you could do is try to get along. Sharing is caring. You said it yourself, we're a team, remember?"

He gives me the stink eye like a toddler who didn't get his way and walks ahead of me. I must have hit a nerve.

After taking the elevator to each of the sixty floors and Hairy Mac uses his bizarre demon tracking skills, there's no sign of Layla. Getting in the elevator, we head back down to the main floor and then rush across the glass-covered skywalk to the second tower.

Hours later, I sit in the hallway on the sixtieth floor exhausted, ready to throw in the towel for the day. Hairy Mac is on all fours sniffing the bottom of the doors of the rooms like a mad dog.

He stands up and his comb-over flops down his nose, making him cross-eyed. "No demons are here."

I'm ready to fight the son of a bitch. If the Dog-God hadn't interfered, I'd have Layla, and she'd be safe. I give him a murderous glare and climb to my feet. "They've probably left the resort. They could be anywhere. Eff, you, this is your fault." I stomp away to stop myself from kicking him in the nuts.

At the elevator, the beast's heavy footsteps come up behind me. It occurs to me, that something Jenny Favor said. I turn and look at him. "There's an open-air rooftop lounge in this tower that only A-listers know about. Layla could still be here." With a glimmer of hope, I jab the 'up' button.

On the top floor, the elevator opens into a short corridor with a glass door at the end, leading to the rooftop lounge. I glance at Hairy Mac with his nose wrinkled up in the air, sniffing, like he's hot on the trail of his prey.

"I smell six demons," he tells me.

My pulse cranks up a notch.

Snatching my gun from the holster, I peer through the door. It's dark out. The rooftop lounge would be a cool hangout on a normal basis. The twinkling lights coming from the city are strikingly beautiful in contrast to the reality of the slum-pit streets below. My eyes dart around the lounge. In the corner, next to one of the large-scale sculptures of a dolphin, I spot Layla sitting at one of the bar tables. Relief overwhelms me. It was a long shot. I never expected to find her again.

The twins and five unfamiliar faces are standing around a white circular bar, talking. I do the math, and I'm not thrilled with the odds. Seven demons. Four bullets. "I thought you said there were only six demons. There's seven men plus Layla."

Hairy Mac presses his face against the glass like a little kid. "Arioch is a sadistic monster from Level Eight. Balam in his true form has three heads. The ugly fool thinks he can predict the future."

Shaking my head, I can't believe I'm part of this carnival side-show. "What about the twins and the others?"

"The twins aren't that special. The other two are low-level Hellions." He peers through the glass again. "What is he doing here?"

"Who?"

"Lucifer's brother, Michael."

My mind goes blank for several seconds then recognition kicks me in the gut. "Michael the Archangel?"

"The one and only."

I gulp hard. Six demons plus the powerful leader of God's army, the chief angel who defeated Lucifer, thrown in as a bonus. This is epic shit. "What does he have to do with this?"

"He's always had a chip on his shoulder, jealous of Lucifer's popularity. Lately, more souls have been entering Hell than Heaven since Lucifer implemented some improvements to make it more attractive. Happy souls, happy afterlife. It's all a numbers game. He'll fight Lucifer until the end of times."

I scratch my head. "For the life of me, I can't figure out how Layla is involved."

"I don't know what game Michael is playing. He's a troublemaker."

"I'll get Layla out of the resort and back to her father." Years of practicing at the shooting range had better not fail me now.

"Aim for the heart. Don't waste a shot on Michael. Only an archangel can kill him, like Lucifer."

"You had better step up your game and show me what you've got," I say with ball-breaking testosterone. "Layla's life is at stake."

Hairy Mac's body stretches, distorts, and twists. Then his shirt and pants rip apart. The Dog-God crawls out, shedding his human host onto the floor. He shakes his head and gobs of slobber slap against my jacket. "They know we're here."

My throat tightens, and I feel a terror like I've never felt before. Clutching the gun, I let out a shuttered breath and open the door.

CHAPTER FIVE

Hairy Mac sprints ahead of me. He leaps over a row of tables, growling and baring his teeth. Landing on all fours in front of Michael, his muscles bulge twice the size.

Adrenaline surges through my veins. Two-handing the gun, I stop a few yards from Layla and keep the weapon trained on the group.

"Hairy Mac. Well, isn't this fun. I was wondering when you'd show up to the party," Michael says and cracks his knuckles.

The dog lunges, snarling. "I should have known you had something to do with this. Go back to where you belong."

Snatching up tables and chairs, the demon crew begins throwing them over the side of the building. They move behind Michael, spreading out in a vee, setting the stage for all hell to break loose.

Fear rises in the back of my throat. My gaze darts from the twins to the chief angel. His dark brown hair and chiseled features look fake like shiny plastic under the moonlight.

Michael glares at me with piercing blue eyes. "Who are you?"

"Chase Decker. I'm taking Layla home to her father."

He rolls his eyes. "How cute."

Layla abruptly stands, her voice red-hot with fury. "You will never have my father's throne. He won't allow it."

"Don't be too sure about that. Many of his minions have turned against him and in time, more will follow once word spreads. We're going to take over Hell and my dear brother will be exiled to Earth to live out the rest of his days tormented by his own kind. How ironic."

"You can't do this. He's, my father." Tears well up in her eyes. "Please, I'm begging you."

Blood roars in my ears and all I care about is Layla. Thinking I should reach for her, I stop myself, afraid to make a sudden move that could accelerate things.

Too late.

Michael flicks both arms straight out in front of him like he's throwing something at me.

A gust of wind sends me back across the rooftop. Fighting to stay upright, the soles of my shoes heat up and start to smoke. Stomping my feet like a mad man, I shove against the air, barely able to move forward a couple of inches at a time.

Hairy Mac's ears go back, and his tail turns ramrod straight. He lunges again at Michael. "Enough with the games. You're nothing more than a pathetic fool. Your longing to be accepted is no more than a desperate cry for help. Lucifer will always be better than you. Time for you to go home, asshole."

That's my cue. The fine hairs on my arms stand up.

The rooftop turns into a mosh pit of pandemonium. Furniture flies in every direction. One of the demons lifts a heavy life-sized dolphin statue and chucks it at me. It misses me by a yard, hits the ground, and smashes into pieces. Finally free from the savage wind, I sprint around the table to Layla, and at the same time raise the weapon and shoot Arioch. The slug drills into his heart. His body erupts into flames, and he disappears.

One down. Six to go.

Michael points at Hellion #1. "Get the girl!" He hurls a fireball at me shooting from his hand.

Seriously? A friggin fireball? I duck and dodge the fast-moving bundle of orange and red flames. Landing in a tree at the end of the rooftop, fire licks up the trunk and spreads to the tree next to it. Pivoting, I watch Hairy Mac brutally attacks Balam using his immense paws, flattening him to the ground. He sinks his teeth into the demon's chest and with one bite, tears out his heart. An explosion of light bursts from his body, and then he's gone.

A squeaky voice slices through the chaos. "Use your wings as shields. Protection mode."

Nothing like learning an important detail this late in the game. "You could have told me earlier," I mumble under my breath.

Layla pounds a fist down on the table and directs her anger at Michael, now hovering above, laughing, as his snow-white gold-tipped wings flap around him. "You cut my wings from my body so I can't ever fly again. You clipped them like I'm a bird. How could you do that to me? You're my uncle."

The news guts me. I'm horrified and fuming that he hurt her.

"Lucifer is going to make you pay for this," Hairy Mac growls and scrambles after Scarface's twin. He snatches one of his legs and tosses him off his feet. Dragging his victim on his back past me, he claws at him, shredding his skin and muscles.

Scarface's beady eyes narrow. Gigantic black wings emerge from his back and flare. He comes at me headfirst like an NFL linebacker and pushes me back...and back...and off the friggin roof.

I plummet, spinning like a top.

Freaking out, my wings open. Dizzy and unable to get my bearings, my blood pumps faster, and I flap madly.

I keep tumbling.

A hundred feet from the ground, I gain control and swoop to the top of the tower with new resolve. No one pushes me over the edge. And no one hurts Layla.

Landing back on the rooftop and out of breath, I observe Hellion #1 seize Layla's arm. She slaps at him, fighting to free herself.

I spring into action.

Aiming for his heart, I swear I'm in a movie. Everything seems to be in slow motion, even the round exiting from my gun, traveling at a snail's pace. The piece of lead speeds up and drills through the demon's heart. Another one bites the dust. Out of the corner of my eye, I spot Hairy Mac with Scarface's twin's bloody heart half hanging out of his mouth. He viciously shakes it and spits it out. I swallow hard to stop from puking.

Scarface's blue eyes flicker to bright red. With barely a second or two before he reveals his true self, I shoot. The bullet bores into the sweet spot of his chest and he detonates into a giant blazing inferno.

Above me, razor-sharp feathers like missiles shoot from Michael's wings and rain down.

I pull Layla to the ground, protecting her with my wings. The deadly feather projectiles clink against my wings like metal hail.

She looks up at me and stares blankly. "We have to stop him. He's out of control."

I realize there's still one more demon to deal with and one bullet. "But how?"

She gives a desperate shrug. "No one prepared me for this."

Zila sure didn't warn me about this kind of shitshow.

"Come out, come out, wherever you are," Michael calls out in a childish singsong voice then roars laughing.

At the same time, I catch a whiff of smoke. "I'm getting you out of here."

Two ear-piercing sharp yelps that sound like a wounded animal puncture the air, and another one, and another. Then silence.

My heart stops at the tortured cries.

The color drains from Layla's face. "He's hurting Hairy Mac."

Clamping my jaw, I reach into my jacket pocket and hand her the key card. "When I stand up, get behind my wings. Then when I say run, run for your life. My suite's on the sixtieth floor, tower one."

She gives a small nod and shoves the card into her bra.

"It's going to be okay," I say, trying to reassure her even though I don't believe my own words. It's going to take a miracle to get us out of this.

Michael's voice roars across the universe. "Come on, Chase. The party isn't over. It's just getting started."

One fireball then two, crash against my wings and I hear sizzling like bacon cooking. I stand my ground with all my strength, cocooning Layla.

"Be careful." She kicks off her high heels and her eyes meet mine wide with fear. "I don't want to lose you."

I grab her hand and kiss it. "I'll be okay." Exhaling a shaky breath, I let go of her hand and mentally prepare myself. This had better work. With Hairy Mac down, I'm running out of options.

Rising slowly hunched over, Layla slips under my wings and behind me. When I'm standing straight, I spot Michael levitating high above the city.

"About time you showed up," he shouts. "Are you as wimpy as the so-called Dog-God of the Underworld? He's always been a joke."

My gaze snaps to Hellion #2, looming over Hairy Mac with his back to me. The dog is on his side, and he isn't moving. The demon turns. His fatty mouth curves slowly into a menacing grin and his nostrils flare. He charges at me like a raging bull. I fire the last round and tell Layla to run.

The slug rips into the Hellion's heart and lights him up better than a strobe light show at a rock concert. Demon combustion at its finest. It doesn't get better than this.

"Put me down!"

I whip around, startled by Layla's voice. Michael has one hand around her neck, lifting her off the rooftop.

"*Layla!*" I take off flying,

Dangling in the air, she kicks and punches at him. Moments later, her body goes limp.

Flapping furiously to get to her, a man's deep base voice thunders in high definition. "MICHAEL!"

* * *

A tsunami of emotions rips through me. Ignoring the disembodied voice, I pump my wings with inhuman stamina and speed.

"Father? Why do you always have to ruin all my fun?" Still suspended, Michael glances at Layla's lifeless body, dangling.

Am I hearing things? God? His voice doesn't give me an ounce of comfort. Heaving in gulps of air, I race toward the chief angel, wanting to bust his head open for what he's done to Layla.

"Leave the hybrid alone," God says. "This battle with your brother must stop. It's gone on for too long."

"He started it. Did you forget about the war he caused? I haven't."

"The past must remain where it belongs. Killing the hybrid isn't going to solve a thing. It's only going to make Lucifer angrier, and he'll send out his army. You are the only one who can break the cycle."

"We don't like human-archangel hybrids, or have you forgotten that too? I swear you're becoming senile. Perhaps, it's time for you to step down."

"Hybrid or not, you and your brother need to work things out. Your private archangel club is what's driving this hatred and your actions could prompt a war of all humanity. It's 2027. This behavior is unacceptable."

When I'm almost to Michael, his eyes connect with mine. He smirks and with the flick of his hand unleashes another windstorm.

Birds spiral and drop.

The violent air slams at my body and I struggle to keep my wings moving. Cradling Layla closer against my chest, for a split second, I swear I'm going to fall out of the sky.

"Stop this!" God orders, his voice blaring like a sonic boom around me.

The wind instantly evaporates, and I'm able to maneuver my wings properly again.

"Father, you're such a drama queen. I didn't see you get involved when the little trickster Gabriel was giving us a hard time. You treat all of us differently. Lucifer has always been your pet even though I'm older and more accomplished. He can have his half-breed." Michael lets out a sinister laugh and opens his hand.

Layla drops.

I free-fall into a dive.

Swooping below her, I catch her in my arms, mere yards from the top of the replica Eiffel Tower. Her skin is cool against mine. Peering down at her pale face, she looks so innocent. The outline of Michael's large hand imprint and nasty dark bruises shadow her neck. Her eyes are closed, and she's as limp as a wet noodle. I refuse to think the worst. The fear of losing her before I get to know her squeezes my lungs, and I can barely breathe.

I soar higher.

Holding Layla tighter to my chest, I press two fingers to her throat. No pulse. I pray to the God who allowed Lucifer to steal my rightful place in Heaven, to save her.

Flying aimlessly, unsure what to do, my arms feel like hundred-pound weights. I suck in a breath and fight through the pain. I don't know what I expected to happen by praying. Fighting back tears, I whisper. "Please open those beautiful eyes. I know why I'm in Hell. I'm here because of you. You are my destiny." Reality crashes down on me. Layla's dead. Nothing's going to change that.

Behind me, I hear wings flapping and my muscles tense. Rage like I've never experienced before surges through every part of my body. I refuse to stop and face the archangel. "You killed her. Layla had nothing to do with your childish war with your brother. I'm going to hunt you down and kill you with my bare hands."

"Surprise, asshole. You thought I was dead."

CHAPTER SIX

My heart stops for the second time. *Hairy Mac? How?* I make a quick U-turn and speed toward him, my wings ferociously slicing the air. "She's dead—Michael killed her—I don't know what to do."

"Calm down," he says.

"How can I be calm?" I scream at him and hold out Layla's limp body, feeling completely helpless. "Look at her, she's dead."

Hairy Mac puts a paw over her heart.

"What are you doing?"

"Bringing her back."

"You can do that?"

"I told you I can do anything that Lucifer can."

Bright white and blue light bursts from Layla's chest and swirls through her whole body. At the same time, thunder cracks and lightning flashes across the sky.

Her eyes slowly open and she looks up at me through tangled hair.

I've never felt so grateful in my life for a second chance. "You're alive." Brushing a strand of hair out of her face, I gently kiss her cheek.

The Dog-God removes his paw and stares at me. "You owe me, asshole."

I start laughing.

Layla turns and looks at Hairy Mac. "I was really worried about you. I know how strong Michael's powers are. Did he hurt you badly?"

"I'm okay. They thought I was down for the count. I was playing dead, a little trick I learned."

"Playing dead? That's a good one." I notice Layla's eyes are a different color. "Your eyes. They're gold. I don't understand."

"That's because she's born of an archangel and a human," Hairy Mac explains. "She's been brought back to life, reborn."

"What about my wings?" Layla asks.

"Like brand new, Buttercup."

"I can't believe Michael did this to me. I'll never forgive him." Her eyes dart back and forth. "Where is he?"

"Gone," I tell her, relieved for all of us. "Good riddance."

The dog's eyes shift to Layla. "Your father isn't going to be happy about what's going on between you and the asshole, just saying."

"You know I love you but I'm not a child. My father needs to back off. I'm capable of making my own decisions."

"He's only trying to protect you from outside forces. Michael is one of many. You're the daughter of the Prince of Darkness and a hybrid. That puts you at risk. The only place you will be safe is in Hell."

"I'm not going home. I have friends here."

"Like the Italian Stallion?" I blurt out, then regret sounding like a jealous idiot.

"You mean Marcus?" She laughs. "He's just a friend, a national poker star. He donates his winnings to the tent cities to make sure people are fed regularly. Believe me, he hates the self-serving rich crowd and loves taking their money."

I guess I was wrong again. Talk about feeling like a complete heel for misjudging the do-gooder.

Layla smiles at me, her eyes never leaving mine. "Hairy Mac, my father doesn't have a say in this, not this time."

She rolls out of my arms and drops.

Her wings open and she soars at high speed, riding the currents, her gray, white-tipped feathers glistening under the moonlight.

I curse the heavens at having to take her home. I can't. "Don't make me do this. You heard her, Hairy Mac. She doesn't want to go back." My gut twists at the thought of asking the Dog-God for a favor. He'll never let me live it down. "Please talk to Lucifer. He'll listen to you...I care about her."

"You have a few hours, then Layla must return home. It's for her own good, and yours."

* * *

Back in the suite, I press my naked body against Layla's and wrap my arm around her. I don't remember the last time I felt this happy. I can't let this end. "How'd you get involved with Michael?"

"I had to get away for a few days to figure out who I am after learning I'm a hybrid. All these years, I thought I was a demon, a monster, something evil. I didn't know I had a human mother. I have no idea who she is. My father won't tell me." She lowers her gaze and looks defeated. "He is so overbearing. My father doesn't understand I'm not like him. I have real feelings and dreams. A day after I arrived in Lost Vegas, he cut off my credit card thinking that would force me home. Then Michael showed up and wanted me to go along with his plan to take control of Hell. When I refused, he ordered the demons to chop off my wings so I couldn't alert anyone about what was going on. Arioch continued to report to my father, convincing him it was me who wanted his throne. It was all Michael's big fat lie."

I kiss her forehead. "I'm sorry they hurt you."

She leans up on one elbow and her eyes search mine. "Are you going to take me back?"

Her question lodges in my throat and I feel like I'm going to choke. I'm in uncharted territory, with no idea what to do. No one wins except for Lucifer. "If I return without you, your father will have my head. If I take you home, there's no way he's going to let us see each other."

"I know he won't allow it." She lets out a sigh. "This is embarrassing. I've never gone on a real date, or even had a boyfriend."

The anguish on her face is killing me. I've never felt like this about a woman. All I want to do is hold her and protect her forever.

A shadow crosses her face, and she sits up. "I'm not going home. I have my wings back and we can go anywhere."

"He'll hunt us down. We'll always be on the run," I tell her.

Her hand moves slowly up my chest, and I shudder at her touch. My body reacts instantly for the third time.

"I've missed out on a lot because I'm Lucifer's daughter. I'm not missing out on anything ever again." She pauses for a beat. "Did you mean what you said about being your destiny?"

I'm busted. "You heard me?"

She nods. "Your voice sounded far away, but I could make out what you were saying. You were worried about me. I feel the same way about you. I believe fate has brought us together."

"I meant every word." I tilt her chin upward slightly and kiss her slowly, savoring each delicious sensation. Suddenly, I stop at the sound of footsteps. Crazy alert. *Not now!*

"What's wrong?"

"We've got company. Hairy Mac." Scrambling, I hand her my t-shirt from the floor, and she hastily pulls it on.

An overly tanned woman in her forties with light brown hair in a high ponytail appears in the doorway of the bedroom dressed in a blue uniform. "We need to talk."

I can't stop grinning at his choice of a new demon body. "Why are you in a woman's body dressed like a maid? Trying to make a couple of extra bucks on the side?"

"You've got the key card."

"Did you ever think to knock?"

"Never crossed my mind, asshole."

Layla grabs my hand and straightens her spine. "I already told you. I'm not going home."

"Your father is not pleased. I spoke with him."

"I don't care. This isn't about him. For once in my life, it's about me, what I want. I'm staying."

She's amazing. I can't help smiling at her unwavering defiance to regain control of her life. She deserves to be happy.

"He said you can stay," Hairy Mac announces.

"Are you serious?" Layla glances at me. "What about Chase?"

Time seems to drag on forever. He's taking his sweet time on purpose to watch me sweat. I'm on the verge of screaming at him.

"The asshole can stay."

The tension in my body fades and my heart soars. I squeeze Layla's hand.

"Zila will arrive tomorrow to give you both additional training. If you're going to stay in Lost Vegas, you'll need it." The Dog-God stares at me, his female voice ice-cold. "If anything happens to her, Lucifer will cut off your teeny-weeny family jewels. After that you'll have to deal with me."

"I won't let you or Lucifer down. You have my word."

"Thank you." Layla's face lights up. "This means

the world to me, Hairy Mac. You're the best. I love you."

"I think I'm blushing. Yuck. Girl stuff," the Dog-God says. "Got to get out of this girly body before I puke. If you need anything, you know where to find me. Stay safe, Buttercup."

After Hairy Mac leaves, Layla's eyes gloss over with tears. "I never thought this day would come. I can't believe it. I'm free."

We both are. "I know you've never been on a date but...how about a cozy booth, a bottle of Dom, and dinner?"

"I'd love to."

I hesitate for a moment and wrangle all my courage. "I'm not going to lie. I'm falling hard for you. No matter what happens, I will always protect you. And love you."

A soft, sexy whisper escapes her lips. "For eternity?"

"For eternity," I say, and kiss her with everything I've got.

AUTHOR NOTE

I hope have you enjoyed reading Hell's Bounty Hunter. Be sure to leave a review! Love reading post-apocalyptic dystopian novels? Don't forget to check out the thrilling Sum of all Tears Series (Icehaven and Liberty)! "Fans of apocalyptic stories looking for a change from tales of melting ice caps will enjoy this cooler treat." (BookLife)

Want to learn more about the Kim?
Visit www.kimcresswell.ca

OTHER BOOKS BY KIM CRESSWELL

Whitney Steel Series

Reflection (Book 1)

Retribution (Book 2)

Resurrect (Book 3)

Raina Storm Series

Dawn of the Storm (Book 1)

Dawn of the Enemy (Book 2)

Assassin Chronicles Series

Deadly Shadow (Book 1)

Sum of all Tears Series

Icehaven (Book 1)

Liberty (Book 2)

Emergence Saga Series

Seeking Hope (Book 1)

Single Title Novellas

Lethal Journey

Hell's Bounty Hunter

True Crime Quickie Short Stories

Real Life Evil

Murder on Sunset Strip

Garden of Bones

Edge of Madness

Chameleon

Backwoods Murder